My Family
My
Mom and Dad

by Claudia Harrington
illustrated by Zoe Persico

Looking Glass Library

An Imprint of Magic Wagon
abdopublishing.com

To my wonderfully wacky family. Special thanks also to Meg Kuroyanagi. —CH

To all of my aunts, uncles, and cousins for the endless support and love. —ZP

abdopublishing.com

Published by Magic Wagon, a division of ABDO, PO Box 398166, Minneapolis, Minnesota 55439. Copyright © 2016 by Abdo Consulting Group, Inc. International copyrights reserved in all countries. No part of this book may be reproduced in any form without written permission from the publisher. Looking Glass Library™ is a trademark and logo of Magic Wagon.

Printed in the United States of America, North Mankato, Minnesota.
052015
092015

THIS BOOK CONTAINS
RECYCLED MATERIALS

Written by Claudia Harrington
Illustrated by Zoe Persico
Edited by Heidi M.D. Elston
Designed by Candice Keimig

Library of Congress Cataloging-in-Publication Data

Harrington, Claudia, 1957- author.
  My mom and dad / by Claudia Harrington ; illustrated by Zoe Persico.
    pages cm. -- (My family)
  Summary: "Lenny follows Kan for a school project and learns what it's like to have a multicultural family"-- Provided by publisher.
  ISBN 978-1-62402-107-7
1. Japanese Americans--Juvenile fiction. 2. Families--Juvenile fiction. 3. Japan--Social life and customs--Juvenile fiction. [1. Japanese Americans--Fiction. 2. Family life--Fiction. 3. Japan--Social life and customs--Fiction. 4. Youths' art.] I. Persico, Zoe, 1993- illustrator. II. Title.
  PZ7.1.H374Mr 2016
  [E]--dc23
                                    2015002663

"Hi, Lenny!" said a boy after the last bell.

"I'm Kan, rhymes-with-Don. I'm Student of the Week!"

"Hi," said Lenny.

Click!

"How do you get home?"

Kan hummed "The Wheels on the Bus."

Both boys laughed.

The bus dropped them off
in front of Kan's house.
Click!

When they walked in, Kan slid off his shoes and put on slippers.

"Who taught you to do that?" asked Lenny.

"My mom. It's a Japanese custom," said Kan. "Do you mind?"

"If you don't mind stinky socks." Lenny grinned.

Lenny's stomach rumbled. "Who gets your snack?"

"My mom," said Kan. "Hi, Mom! We're starving! Hey, Mikey!"

"This is Lenny," said Kan.
Click!
Kan's mom smiled. "Nice to meet you, Lenny-kun."
"Hi," said Lenny.

Lenny turned to Kan. "What does that *kun* thing mean?"

"It's an old-fashioned way of saying you're a friend." Kan elbowed Lenny and handed him some chopsticks. "Want to try these for fun?"

"Oops!" said Lenny. A grape rolled across their work sheets.

"Let one rest on your fourth finger," said Kan, demonstrating.

"Your thumb and first two fingers grab the other one."

"Who taught you that?" asked Lenny.

"My dad," said Kan. "He can do it with both hands, like a crab!"

Click!

Lenny accidentally launched a grape at Kan's head.

They cracked up.

"Is it okay if I use my fingers?" Lenny asked.

"Yes-o-rama," said Kan. "But you'll get it, if you practice.

You can keep those."

"Thanks," said Lenny. "Do you always eat with chopsticks?"

"Most of the time. But we use spoons and stuff, too." Kan smiled.

"It's hard to eat ice cream with chopsticks!"

When they finished their homework, they headed to Kan's room.
Click!

14

"Whoa!" said Lenny, tapping on the drums.

"Go for it, Lenny. Let's jam!" Kan grabbed a guitar and rocked out.

"Wow," said Lenny. He hit the snare.
"Who taught you how to play? You're good."
"My dad. He played lead guitar for the
Maddest Hatters."
"Cool!" said Lenny.

"Hey, my turn," said Kan.
Click!

17

Kan's mom poked her head in.
"Let's give Lenny-kun a little concert."
"Mo-om," said Kan as his mom
dragged a cello and a koto out
of the closet.

"Awesome!" said Lenny. "Where did you learn how to play the cello?"

"From my mom!" answered Kan.

"What's that long thing?" asked Lenny.

"It's a koto, a Japanese instrument," said Kan. "Mom is really good."

"Hey, buddy," said Kan's dad. "Jam session still open?"

"Abso-posi-lutely!" Kan flung himself at his dad.

"Even more awesome!" said Lenny.
Click!

Kan's mom smiled. "Any hungry musicians in the house?"

"Yes!" said Lenny, Kan, and Kan's dad.

Mikey clapped and jumped up and down.

"As long as I don't have to use these." Lenny held up the drumsticks, and they all laughed.

Lenny whispered to Kan, "Are we having sushi? I'm not sure about raw fish." Kan grinned. "Don't worry. It's BBQ night!"

"Who makes your dinner?" asked Lenny.

"My dad's lighting up the grill tonight.

He's making ribs!" said Kan.

Click!

"Hey, Lenny," said Kan after dinner, "want to make an origami cricket until your mom gets here? It's the coolest origami thing I know how to make."

"Meatloaf can have a friend!" said Lenny.

"Meatloaf?" asked Kan.

"My pet cricket," said Lenny.
Click!

"Who taught you origami?" asked Lenny.

"My mom," said Kan, yawning. "Origami is a super-old Japanese thing."

"Who reads your bedtime story?" asked Lenny.

"My dad, sort of. He sings me ballads. You know, sleepy songs."

"Lenny," called Kan's dad, "your mom's here."

"Sorry to break this up, boys," said Lenny's mom.

"Just one more question, Kan," said Lenny. "Who loves you best?"

"We do!" said Kan's parents. **Click!**

29

Student of the Week

Kan

Lenny grinned. "Meatloaf says he loves me, too! See you tomorrow, rock star!" Kan laughed. "Stay cool, Lenny-kun."